The Chaos Shark

AMY LAURENS

OTHER WORKS

Find other works by the author at www.amylaurens.com

The Chaos Shark

INKLET #76

AMY LAURENS

Inkprint PRESS

www.inkprintpress.com

Print ISBN: 978-1-922434-16-6
eBook ISBN: 9798201815431

www.inkprintpress.com

National Library of Australia Cataloguing-in-Publication Data
Laurens, Amy 1985 –
The Chaos Shark
38 p.
ISBN: 978-1-922434-16-6
Inkprint Press, Canberra, Australia
1. Fiction—Fantasy—Contemporary 2. Fiction—Fairy Tales, Folk Tales, Legends & Mythology 3. Fiction—Short Stories

First Print Edition: February 2022
Cover photo © Sarah Richter via Pixabay
Cover design © Inkprint Press
Interior art © Amy Laurens

THE CHAOS SHARK

I WAS SICK OF WATCHING DAD AND Nathan fish. Sick of cataloguing what they caught, sick of the smell of prawns and salt, sick of the unsettling motion of the waves. But the last straw came when Nathan downed his can of Coke and threw it over the side.

"That's littering," I snapped, watching the red-and-silver can bob in the silky waves.

He shrugged. "Aluminium's biodegradable, isn't it?"

"After like a hundred years," I said, glaring at him. "Where's the net?"

He nodded vaguely to the stern where the green net stood, propped up against the cracked poly-leather of the seats, trying to snare the sun.

"Don't hassle him," Dad said serenely, eyes closed as he dozed in the boat's front seat.

I tshh'd through my teeth. Dad had decided to grow out his beard, and it cascaded down his chest like an avalanche. He looked exactly like the Father Christmas of my toddlerhood—for more reasons than one. Only today, instead of gifts, he bore slimy prawns and squid and pilchards, and false pacifism. "I'm not hassling," I said. "I just want the net."

I scrambled to the back of the boat and snatched it up, testing its weight and length. "Hold me, will you?" I asked Nathan.

He laughed and waved at me with his rod.

I sniffed. Priorities.

I eyed the can, bobbing in the water a good stretch away, then squinted at the net. It would be close. I thought about asking Dad to move the boat for me, but as I opened my mouth Nathan whooped and his line whizzed. I sighed. If he had a fish on I'd be lucky to get the can in at all, and if he got the fish up it'd be all elbows and tromping, and get out of the way, Ellie; I need the net, Ellie; get the fish in the boat, Ellie.

Grinding my teeth, I fed the net out over the swirling, silking water. Almost there, almost… The can danced tantalisingly out of reach, and behind me Nathan swore. "He's gone." I almost *felt* Dad relax back into his seat as the promise of a catch evaporated. I stretched farther.

Swell rocked the boat and without warning I overbalanced, clutching futilely at the gunwales before pitching headfirst into the cold water. I broke the surface and gasped, treading water, net still firmly in hand.

Nathan howled. "I thought you said not to litter," he said, wiping tears from the corners of his eyes.

"Funny," I snapped.

Dad waved an unconcerned hand. "Come on then, get back in."

I glanced at the shore, rock shelves a scant twenty-five metres away. The ocean was lazy today, barely reaching up to touch the rocks before dropping back into itself. I shook my head. "I'll wait for you on the rocks."

Dad shrugged. "Suit yourself."

I passed the net back to Nathan and swam towards the shelf, cutting through the water—I'd learned to swim before I could walk, if you counted floating on my back as swimming. I rolled over and backstroked for a while, watching the puffs of cloud straggle across the sky to the horizon, where they seemed to linger. I bunched my lips. Maybe old Burke was right and we'd get a storm tonight after all.

My fingers grazed the rocks and I flipped over, finding finger- and toe-holds in amongst the barnacles and whelks, the slippery seaweed and sharp-shelled periwinkles.

As I climbed, shells cracked under my bare feet and I winced, imagining a giant foot appearing in the sky to squash me flat. I shook my head to clear the image—but the sense of un-ease stayed, coating my skin like a salty sea-film.

Chewing my lip, I glanced out to sea. The storm might be coming faster than even Burke could predict. I waved my arms and hollered. "Hey! Hey, Dad!"

He waved back, still half asleep, and I stabbed my finger at the horizon. He looked over his shoulder at the gath-ering grey and nodded. The rod next to him gave a jerk and flattened, and I knew the sound so well I imagined I could hear the line scream from here. Dad grinned at me as he snatched up the rod and shrugged.

I rolled my eyes. If the fish were biting, Dad and Nathan would stay out 'til they drowned.

I pursed my lips at the horizon, then decided it wasn't my problem. Dad and Nath were big boys. They'd look after themselves. If nothing else, they'd come in eventually so they didn't lose the fish they'd caught earlier in the day —a handful of chopper tailor and a shiny orange snapper longer than my forearm.

I minced my way over towards the cliff, hoping that if the rain did hit before the boys were finished, it might provide me with some shelter. Dad and Nathan at least had the boat; if the swell decided to really make a go of it, I'd be swept off the rocks and away without a moment's thought. I was a good swimmer, but that didn't make me a match for the ocean in a mood.

A movement ahead caught my eye and I altered my path, frowning at the tide pool whose surface churned oddly. The pool was only a couple of paces across; had a fish got caught in there when the tide had gone out?

I made my way closer, wincing as I sliced my foot on a particularly sharp shell, shifting my weight and wincing again as I snagged my toes on the rocks. I hobbled to the pool, thinking to stand in it for some relief from the sharpness underfoot—and changed my mind.

In the bottom of the pool—half as deep as it was wide—curled a small shark. It gave a flick, tail cutting the surface: the odd churning I'd seen before. I squinted at it, pushing my wet hair out of my face. Definitely a shark, with its triangular dorsal fin, spoked tail, snub nose, and rough, cartilage skin—but a strange shark. The tips of its fins and tail were deepest black; not so unusual, I'd seen sharks with markings like that before once or twice. It was the body colour that made me stare: bright, deep blue, electric like neon lights. I'd seen cloud-coloured sharks and sand-coloured sharks, deep-brown dappled sharks and cold-steel-grey sharks, but never a shark that looked like something out of a nineteen-nineties hypercolour party.

Goose bumps rose on my arms as wind whipped across the shelf.

I shivered and glanced nervously at the horizon. That storm was brewing fast, faster than any storm I could remember.

The shark flicked feebly and sank to settle on the bottom. My pulse skipped as I realised that plastic snagged in the rock pool was twined around the shark's fin. It was dying.

Lightning flashed in the distance,

thunder grumbling on its heels. The waves gnawed hungrily at the rock shelf, kicking up sprays of white.

The shark flicked again and for the briefest instant, the temperature rose and the wind softened to a breeze that smelled of long, hot days and summer sun. As the shark sank again to the sand of the tide pool, the wind roared, hustling the storm clouds closer.

My stomach clenched. "Oh. My gosh." It couldn't be. How was it *possible*? I stared at the shark, stared at the storm, stared back at the shark. I'd heard the rumours, of course, muttered by old folk like Burke, old folk who everyone respected because their knowledge of tides and weather verged on preternatural, but who everyone privately—very privately, though everyone knew that everyone else thought it, that was the way of these things—thought was barmy. Burke had told me once about the chaos sharks, great creatures whose life was connected to the harmony of the ocean, of the world—but I'd been six. It was just a story.

The shark's tail trembled. It didn't matter. The shark was dying; I had to at least try to save it. If that helped the weather, great. If not, well, there was nothing I could do about that anyway. I glanced back out to where Dad and Nathan were frantically reeling in lines and packing away bait and lures. Nothing I could do for them, either—except maybe rescue the shark.

I bit my lip, wondering how to approach this. The first drops of freezing rain splattered against my skin—big, fat drops that promised a torrential downpour.

An engine coughed, spluttered. My gaze darted back to our boat, throat tight. I wasn't sure if I wanted them to leave me here and get to safety, or do something stupid and heroic to save me. But I'd be fine, so long as I didn't go near the edge of the shelf. My eyes slid back to the shark. So long as I didn't approach the water.

The engine coughed again and died. Nathan, hanging out over the stern, shouted something at Dad, both of them waving frantically.

If they couldn't get away before the storm arrived, before the waves rose and dashed them to pieces against the rocks… I choked away the bile in my throat.

The shark. It had stopped moving.

A mighty wave rose, swelling, swelling, swelling, and broke over the rocks, spilling across the shelf. Dad stood at the wheel of the boat, but instead of steering he gripped the gunwales tightly and stared out at the rocky teeth that gaped, longing to catch the boat. Nathan beat frantically at the engine, but it wasn't going to do any good.

Another splatter of rain gusted on the wind and ice bit into my skin. Hailstones, tiny for now, but how big would they grow?

I plunged my arms into the tide pool, salty shallows still warm, and tore at the string of plastic. It took both hands to snap it, but I cleared it away and scooped up the shark. It twitched as though wanting to fight me, but its sides heaved and after a moment it fell still. Even so, I nearly dropped it back into the water as I struggled to balance it in my arms. The water must have created an optical illusion; I was sure the shark had been smaller in the pool. I remembered the images I'd seen of crocodile hunters up north and wrapped the shark around the back of my waist, hugging its head to one hip and its jet black tail to the other.

The wind howled now, ripping at my clothes, my hair. I hefted the shark and stepped towards the ocean. Dad shouted, gesturing frantically at me— go back, go back! But I couldn't. I was committed now, I had the shark in my arms—bloody hell, a real, mostly-live shark—and old Burke had to be right, he just had to, because if he wasn't, Dad and Nathan would be smashed against the rocks and maybe drown, and unless I ran faster than I'd ever run in my life and there was a miracle that slowed the encroaching water, the sea would catch me before I could reach safety.

Burke had to be right. If he wasn't, my family was about to die.

I crept towards the edge of the shelf and the rain spat in my face. Hair tangled in my mouth and I half swallowed it, choking because I couldn't afford to shift my grip on the shark, even for an instant. The wind buffeted me, pushing me back towards the shelf, but I doubled over and staggered, shark over my back, shells slicing my feet, towards the water.

It churned a foot below the edge of the rocks, angry and black and vengeful. My heart hammered. I couldn't go in there. I'd drown.

The shark kicked in my arms as though it knew the water was closer, and once again the smell of summer gusted on the wind. Maybe I could just throw the shark in and make a run for it. I shifted, trying to unwrap the shark from around me without letting it fall, and the wind pushed, and the shark flicked, and I slipped on the seaweed.

The icy shock of the water knocked the wind from my lungs and I thrashed. Where was the surface?

Where were the rocks?

I was going to be smashed against them any moment now, and my chest was burning, and I needed air, air, air, I needed to breathe…

I was going to die.

Something nudged at my back and I grasped at it, pushing myself away, expecting cold, sharp rock. But instead my hands met rough cartilage and an instant later the shark head-butted me again, and I broke the surface, gasping and spluttering, lungs on fire, sinuses burning from the seawater that had flushed through them. I flailed, still fighting for air, and once again my hands met shark—and I wasted the little breath I had on a scream.

The shark was huge. It was the same shark, it had to be—what were the odds another electrically blue shark had turned up right in the nick of time?—but it was twice my length and growing. And, I realised as it swam in slow, small circles with me leaning against its back, the sea was calming. I clung to its fin and half sobbed, half laughed.

Old Burke had been right. Chaos sharks existed. Who knew.

The clouds dissipated and sunlight beamed down. Chest still heaving, I let go of the shark with one hand to flick my hair out of my face. The shark nudged me and I let it go completely, treading water.

"Hey!"

I turned to see Nathan and Dad staring out at me with tight, bloodless faces, hands gripping the gunwale like they might die.

The shark flicked at me with its tail and I laughed. "Shark!" I called, pointing. They didn't seem impressed.

A light breeze swept over the ocean, smelling like hot sand and sunscreen. I ducked my face under the water and blinked about. Empty salt and shadows. The shark was gone.

A thrumming noise made me jerk my head up again.

Nathan had started the engine and they were putting slowly towards me. About a metre away Nathan killed the engine and Dad turned the boat to drift towards me broadside on.

"You okay?" Dad called.

I ducked under once more, but the shark was definitely gone. I surfaced, flinging water out of my face. "Yup," I said. "No problem."

A flash of red caught my eye.

I stroked to the end of the boat, and burst out laughing. Dad and Nathan hurried over, Dad stepping out over the gunwales to the platform by the engine, reaching out for me. I swam to meet him and took his arm, and as he dragged me up I waved my other hand at Nathan. I crumpled the Coke can, splashing seawater everywhere.

"Well," I said, "that'll teach you to litter."

THE MAKING OF
THE CHAOS SHARK

This is a slightly-newer version of an old, old story. The original draft of this story was, in fact, one of the first short stories I wrote, back in the late 2000s when a group of friends and I were trying to learn how to write something shorter than a novel.

Originally, the story was called The Cinnamon Shark, and the eponymous shark was cinnamon-red. The title confused some readers, though, and the story itself had never had quite enough depth and context to work.

So I changed the title to hopefully make the magic a little clearer, and I added the frame around the moment of Ellie (who originally didn't even have a name) finding and releasing the shark.

That story frame, the fishing in the boat with Dad and Nathan, is intimately familiar to me. It recalls countless days spent out on the family boat, deep off shore, with my now-husband's family while we were dating. The Dad and Nathan of the story are, in fact, very similar in my mind to my father- and brother-in-law.

I can still smell the prawns, baking in the hot sun, and the way that salt-and-vinegar chips taste when you're sharing the packet with fishy fingers.

Also... probably don't litter. You just don't want to risk it ;)

Read more by Amy Laurens!

BONES OF THE SEA

THE MAN—WHOSE NAME IS IRRELEVANT, for he hall soon be dead—wandered down the beach where sand whiter than any he'd seen before swashed between a short, head-high cliff to his left, and the frothing waves of the ocean to his right. Salt filled the air, but below that, something else lingered, and he couldn't quite place his... nose... on what it was.

Of course, the locals were horrified that he was here at all. But he was a Man Of Learning, and was not accustomed to heeding the warnings of people obviously less learned than himself, especially when they spoke tales of a beach that left no trespasser alive.

He'd scoffed. Ridiculous, their legends of a beach where to set one toe on the sand was to seal your own death sentence before the rising of the next full moon.

He was far more interested in analysing the sand, quite literally whiter than any he'd seen before, and thus far resistant to his attempts to decode it. He'd thought a pure variety of quartz before he'd arrived, but upon reaching the beach, pulling into the little deserted cul-de-sac dead end festooned with warning signs ('Cursed Beach, Do Not Enter'; 'Beware The Bones Of The Sea'), he'd switched his engine off, opened the car door to the sound of waves and wind through the saltbush, and he'd seen the sharp drop-off down to the sand and had changed his mind to chalk, or maybe gypsum.

But there'd been no tiny fossils his portable microscope could detect, and the sand, whatever it was made from, had failed to fizz under the application of a drop of acid from his little glass vial, so that struck gypsum and chalk from the list of options.

Now, after several hours on the

beach to no avail as the hot evening sun seared his hands and the light glinting off both ocean and white sand blinded him, he'd had enough. He'd run out of fresh water, ideas, and patience all, and was presently hiking back around the cove to his car that glinted silver and tantalising at the far end of the beach, a haven of cool air and fresh water.

Stay. Stay a little while longer.

The salt clung to his skin, filming his lips, the inside of his nose, the back of his throat. Somehow, the ocean smelled sharper here, more concentrated. Briefly, he wondered if that was the source of the townsfolk's rumours; but a higher salt concentration ought to have meant people floated better, drowned less. No. There must simply be a convergence of factors that meant the currents here were particularly treacherous, and indeed, casting his gaze out to the distant horizon, examining the interplay of wave and off-white foam, the cove did seem to be quite swirly, with a few smooth tracts he thought were probably rips.

As ever, folklore had a logical series of explanations behind it.

Just a little longer.

His leather sandal caught on something in the sand.

He stumbled.

Ow. That hurt.

Whatever it was, it had poked through the holes in his footwear to stab at his toes.

Glaring, impatient, our nameless victim kicked away some of the strange, defiant white sand—and inhaled sharply.

Once the initial burst of adrenalin subsided—something a surprise human skull will inevitably inspire, regardless of one's general composure—it seemed obvious.

Of course. The one thing he hadn't

tested for was bone.

So focused on unlocking the mystery of the sand's composition was he that his initial reaction was deep, gleeful satisfaction.

Dawning understanding, however, made him lift his feet, hesitantly at first, shaking the white sand—bone—sand, think of it as sand, it's safer that way—but it's bone, really it's bone, it's all bone, every single grain of it, pure white, sun-bleached bone, spat up from the guts of the ocean the way a predatory owl spits out the bones of its prey—and then his feet were dancing, just like his stomach, as he leapt for the cliff and tried to haul himself up and off the beach because God, oh God, he was standing on bones and only bones, and the skull he'd uncovered had been human, and there, just down the beach, that rock wasn't a rock, it was another skull, and oh God, how many people had died here?

He realised the sobbing was his, rasps of panic as he scrabbled at the embankment that should have been easier to climb than it was, his fingers digging at the rock, skin tearing, sandals scraping for purchase…

Stay.

His back was to the ocean when the freak wave rose, a local tsunami of salt and hunger.

It smashed into him.

As it dragged him out to sea, all he felt was cold, so bitter it froze his bones right in his body.

An hour later, as the sun spilled red-orange lifeblood out over the ocean, the ocean spat a skull, bleached-white and grinning, back up onto the beach. A moment later, as the full moon crested over the craggy headland behind, a sternum—*most* of its ribs still attached—joined the skull, followed a moment later by a single scapula.

And as the moon rose and the ocean

swallowed the sun, a whisper began that sounded like the wind… until you realised there was nothing but salt-bush for the wind to disturb, and the whispers sounded strangely like a voice, hungry, crooning, and singing.

Feed me.

Feeed mee.

Feeeed meeeeee….

AMY LAURENS is an Australian author of fantasy fiction for all ages. She has seen sharks in the wild from the deck of a fishing boat before, but swimming with them was a step too far for comfort.

Amy has also written the award-winning portal-fantasy *Sanctuary* series about Edge, a 13-year-old girl forced to move to a small country town because of witness protection (the first book is *Where Shadows Rise*), the humorous fantasy *Kaditeos* series, following newly graduated Evil Overlord Mercury as she attempts to acquire a castle, the young adult series *Storm Foxes*, about love and magic and family in small town Australia, and a whole host of non-fiction.

INKLETS

Collect them all! Released on the 1st and 15th of each month.

INKLET #079
Shadows NEVER LIE
AMY LAURENS

INKLET #080
Here She Lies
LIANA BROOKS

INKLET #081
Perfect Destruction
An Age Of Unicorns Story
AMY LAURENS

INKLET #082
What Blood Can Do
AMY LAURENS

INKLET #083
Dancer, Dreamer Seer
LIANA BROOKS

INKLET #084
As Time Whirls Slowly Past
AMY LAURENS

INKLET #085
Far More Satisfying Than Hell
AMY LAURENS

INKLET #086
Just Another Day In Hell
LIANA BROOKS

INKLET #087
Moon AND Morning
AMY LAURENS

Some Impropriety Expected
AMY LAURENS

NEON SNOW
LIANA BROOKS

Reincarnation
LIANA BROOKS

More Than Mushrooms
AMY LAURENS

DOUBLE ISSUE
How To Make A Star
& The World Ended
LIANA BROOKS

CAUGHT IN THE ACT
AMY LAURENS

ANUBIS Has Sent You Six Souls
LIANA BROOKS

PRAYER TO A GODDESS
LIANA BROOKS

Love In The Time Of Corona
AMY LAURENS